This book belongs to:
_____

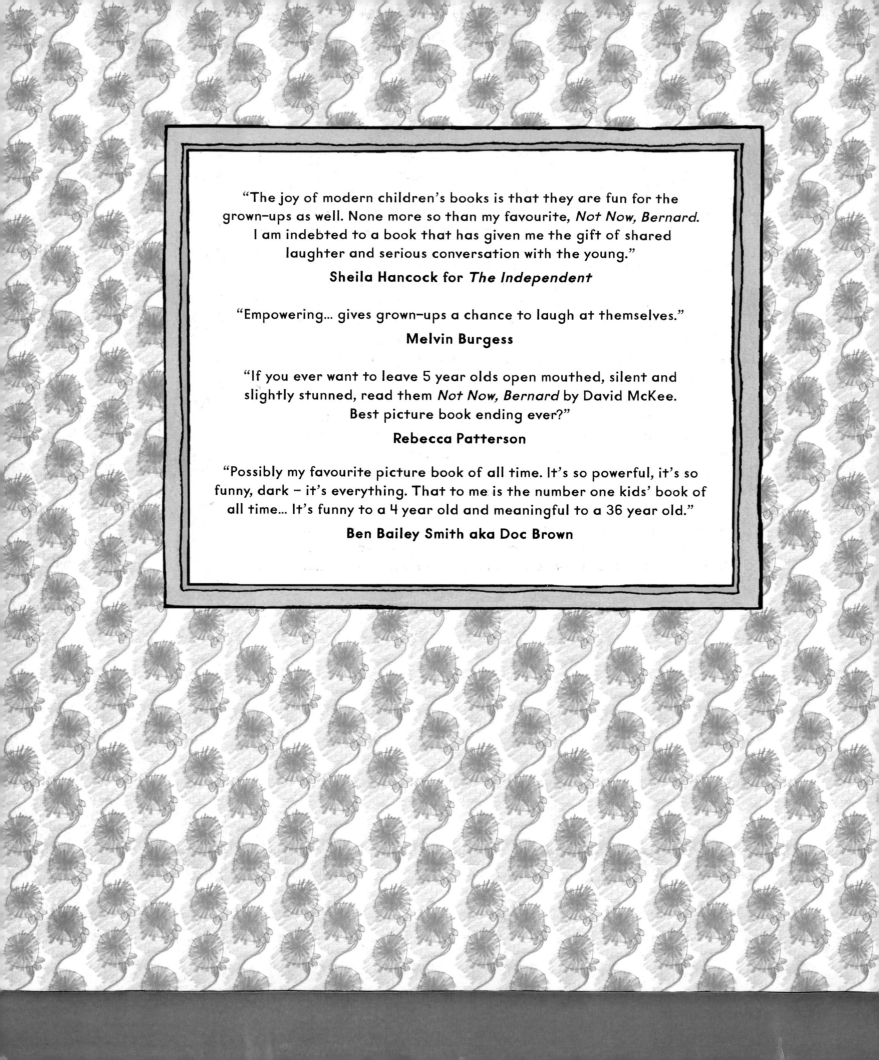

"The joy of modern children's books is that they are fun for the grown-ups as well. None more so than my favourite, *Not Now, Bernard*. I am indebted to a book that has given me the gift of shared laughter and serious conversation with the young."

Sheila Hancock for *The Independent*

"Empowering... gives grown-ups a chance to laugh at themselves."

Melvin Burgess

"If you ever want to leave 5 year olds open mouthed, silent and slightly stunned, read them *Not Now, Bernard* by David McKee. Best picture book ending ever?"

Rebecca Patterson

"Possibly my favourite picture book of all time. It's so powerful, it's so funny, dark – it's everything. That to me is the number one kids' book of all time... It's funny to a 4 year old and meaningful to a 36 year old."

Ben Bailey Smith aka Doc Brown

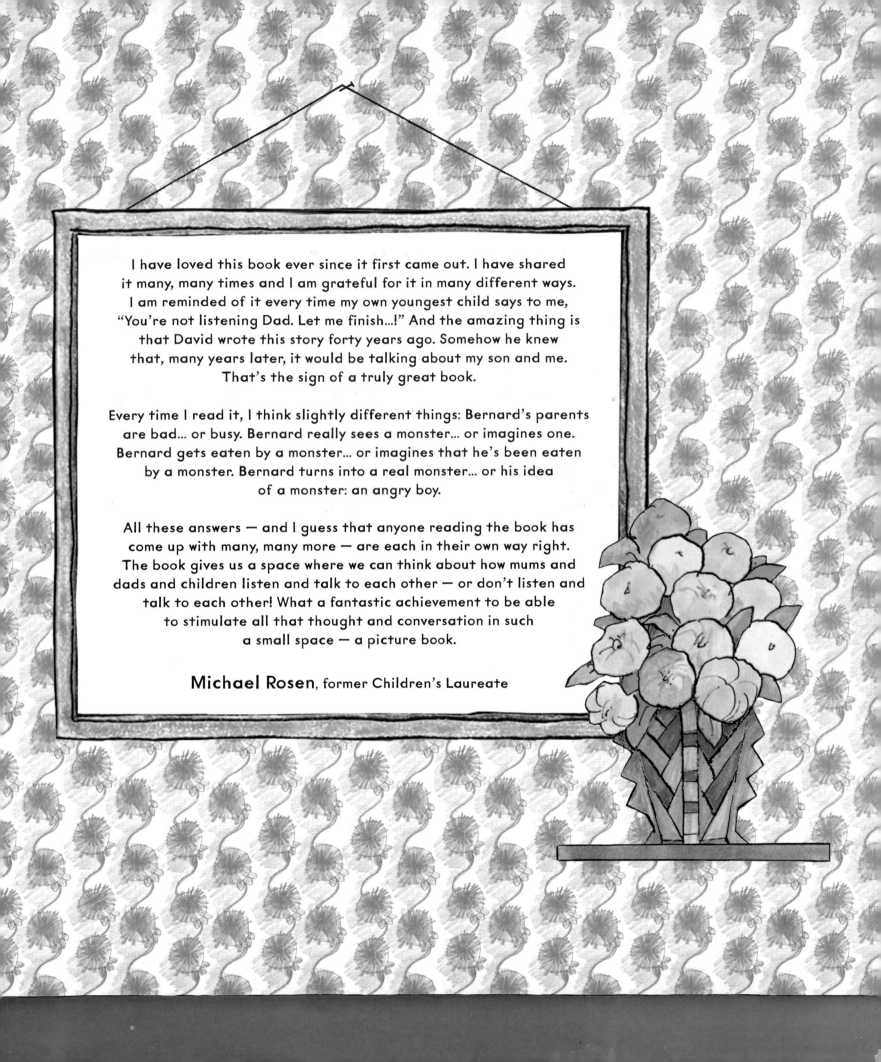

I have loved this book ever since it first came out. I have shared it many, many times and I am grateful for it in many different ways. I am reminded of it every time my own youngest child says to me, "You're not listening Dad. Let me finish...!" And the amazing thing is that David wrote this story forty years ago. Somehow he knew that, many years later, it would be talking about my son and me. That's the sign of a truly great book.

Every time I read it, I think slightly different things: Bernard's parents are bad... or busy. Bernard really sees a monster... or imagines one. Bernard gets eaten by a monster... or imagines that he's been eaten by a monster. Bernard turns into a real monster... or his idea of a monster: an angry boy.

All these answers — and I guess that anyone reading the book has come up with many, many more — are each in their own way right. The book gives us a space where we can think about how mums and dads and children listen and talk to each other — or don't listen and talk to each other! What a fantastic achievement to be able to stimulate all that thought and conversation in such a small space — a picture book.

Michael Rosen, former Children's Laureate

This paperback edition first published in 2020 by Andersen Press Ltd.
First published in Great Britain in 1980 by Andersen Press Ltd.,
20 Vauxhall Bridge Road, London SW1V 2SA.
Copyright © David McKee, 1980.
The right of David McKee to be identified as the author and illustrator of this work has been
asserted by him in accordance with the Copyright, Designs and Patents Act, 1988.
All rights reserved. Printed and bound in China.

1   3   5   7   9   10   8   6   4   2

British Library Cataloguing in Publication Data available.

ISBN 978 1 78344 973 6

NOT NOW, BERNARD

David McKee

Ⓐ

ANDERSEN PRESS

"Hello, Dad," said Bernard.

"Not now, Bernard," said his father.

"Hello, Mum," said Bernard.

"Not now, Bernard," said his mother.

"There's a monster in the garden and it's going to eat me," said Bernard.

"Not now, Bernard," said his mother.

Bernard went into the garden.

"Hello, monster," he said to the monster.

The monster ate Bernard up, every bit.

Then the monster went indoors.

"ROAR," went the monster behind
Bernard's mother.

"Not now, Bernard," said Bernard's mother.

The monster bit Bernard's father.

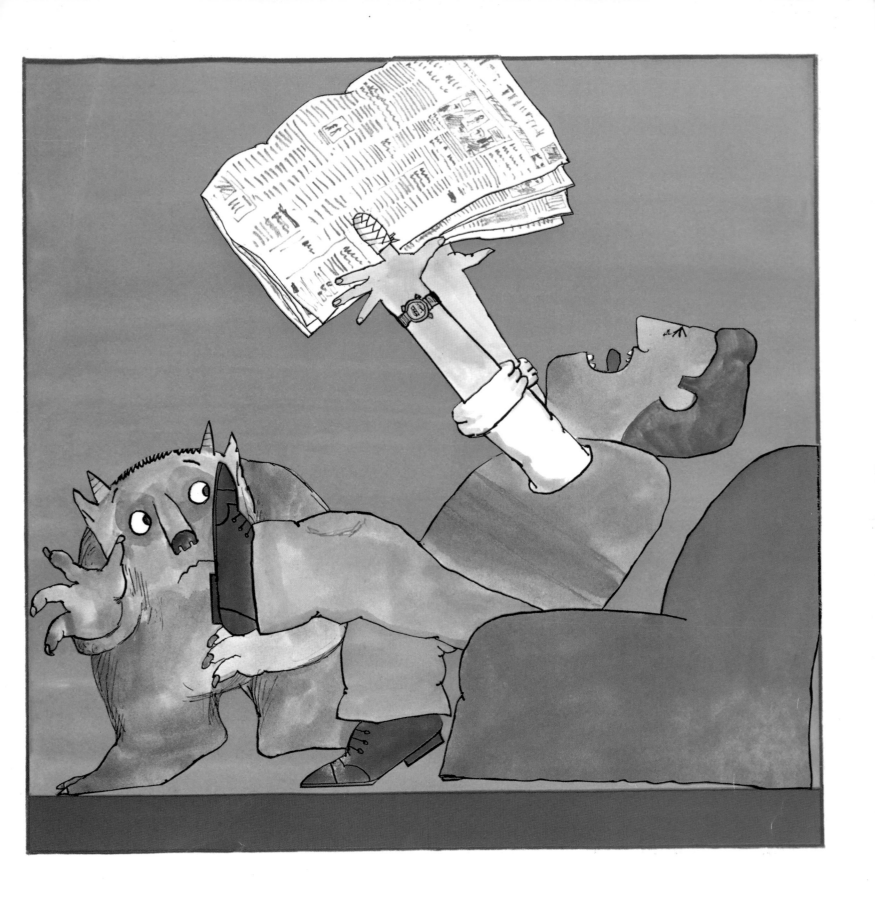

"Not now, Bernard," said Bernard's father.

"Your dinner's ready," said Bernard's mother.

She put the dinner in front of the television.

The monster ate the dinner.

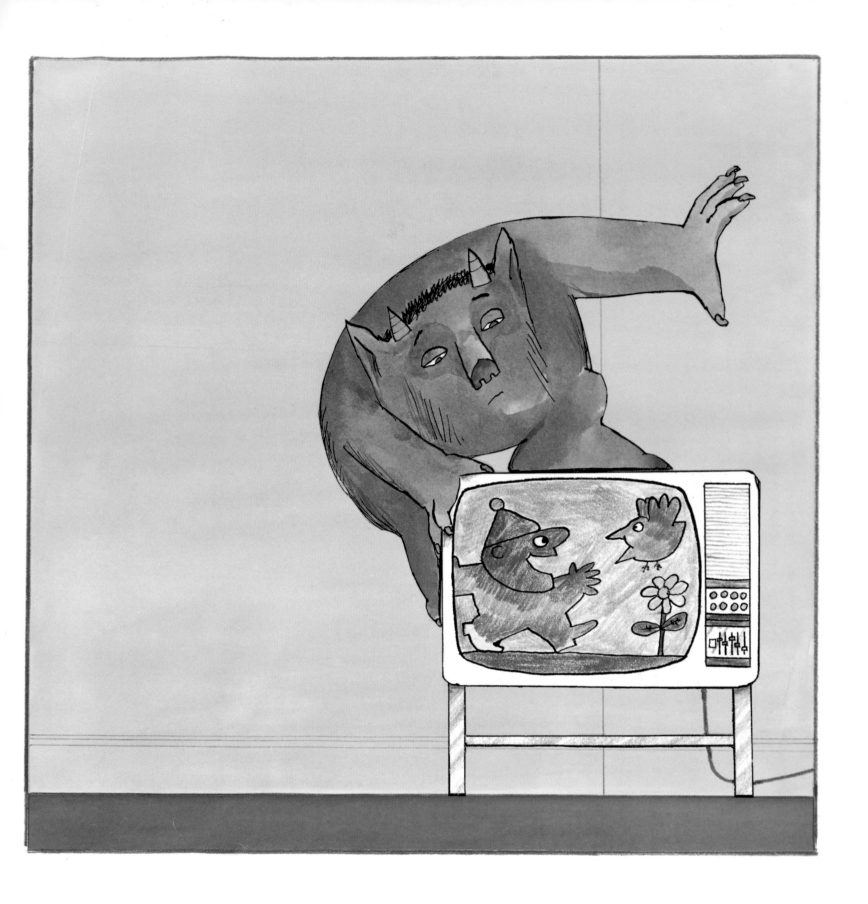

Then it watched the television.

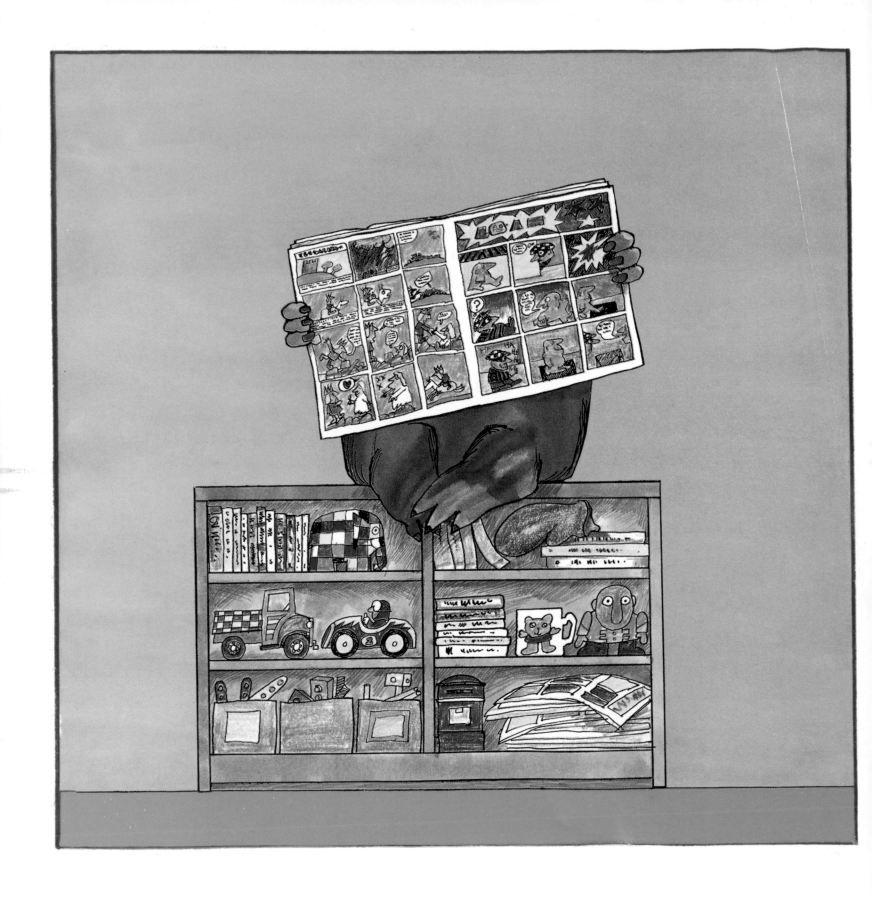

Then it read one of Bernard's comics.

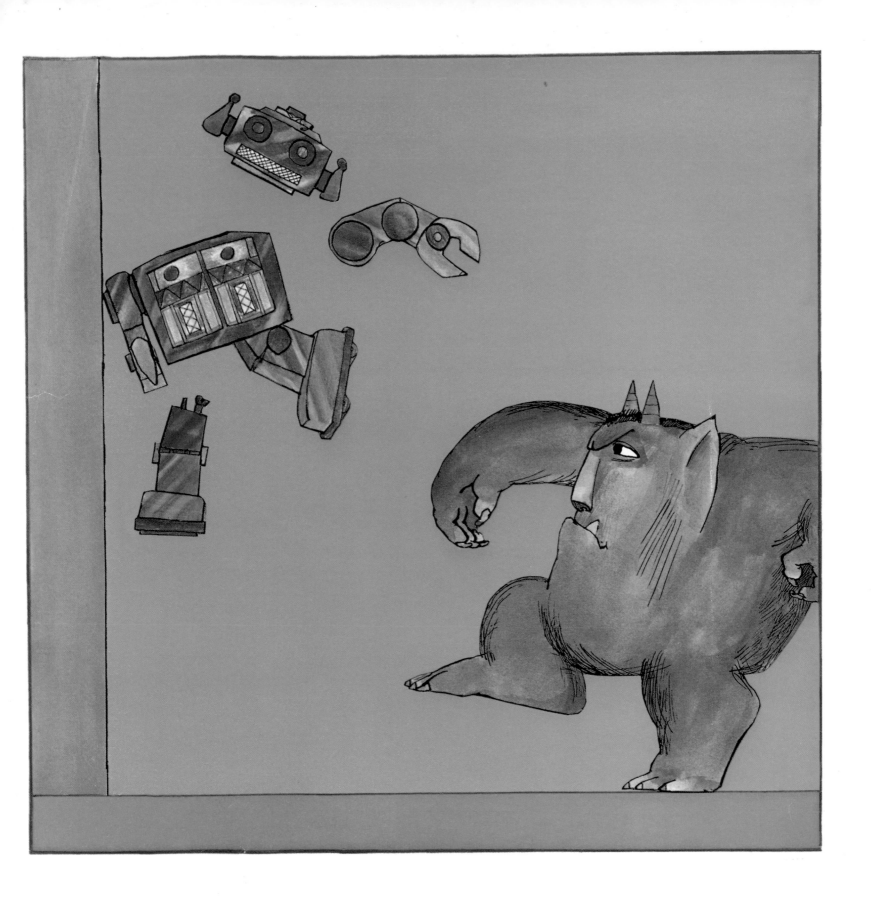

And broke one of his toys.

"Go to bed. I've taken up your milk," called
Bernard's mother.

The monster went upstairs.

"But I'm a monster," said the monster.

"Not now, Bernard," said Bernard's mother.

Sharing this book with children

Not Now, Bernard is a much-loved classic. The havoc caused by the purple monster really appeals to children. Reading about a child who's ignored by his parents can spark interesting questions and conversations, too.

Bernard wants to get his parents' attention but they're always busy. How does this make Bernard feel? Give your child time to think about Bernard's situation. Talking about feelings is a great way to encourage children to open up and make them feel safe.

After eating Bernard, the monster roars at Mum and bites Dad's leg. Why is the monster behaving like this? Talk about how he's acting and why, and whether your child ever feels this way. Look at the pictures and describe what you see.

Bernard and the monster both want to be heard. It can be frustrating for young children to feel like they're not being acknowledged. This is why spending time together, chatting and listening really matters. Sharing a book (or two) every day is a wonderful way to do this.

More information about how to spend quality time together can be found at: **www.actionforchildren.org.uk/notnowbernard**

Sadly, across the UK today, hundreds of thousands of children aren't getting the care and attention they need. Action for Children is working to change this. The charity protects and supports vulnerable children, makes sure their voices are heard and campaigns to bring lasting improvements to their lives.

As part of *Not Now, Bernard*'s anniversary celebrations, Andersen Press has donated to Action for Children to support the charity's vital work and make sure every young person has a safe and happy childhood.

ANDERSEN PRESS

HELPING CHILDREN HAVE SAFE AND HAPPY CHILDHOODS.

Action for Children

 /actionforchildren    @actnforchildren    @actionforchildrenuk

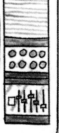

Discover more
DAVID MCKEE
classics...